THE BIG RED BARN

PRF Publishers
Hopewell, New Jersey

Ruth E. Schwinn
www.henrythelamb.com

Library of Congress Control Number: 2009908052

ISBN: 978-0-578-03405-8

Printed in the United States of America

CPSIA Compliance Information: Batch #0809.
For further information contact RJ Communications, NY, NY, 1-800-621-2556

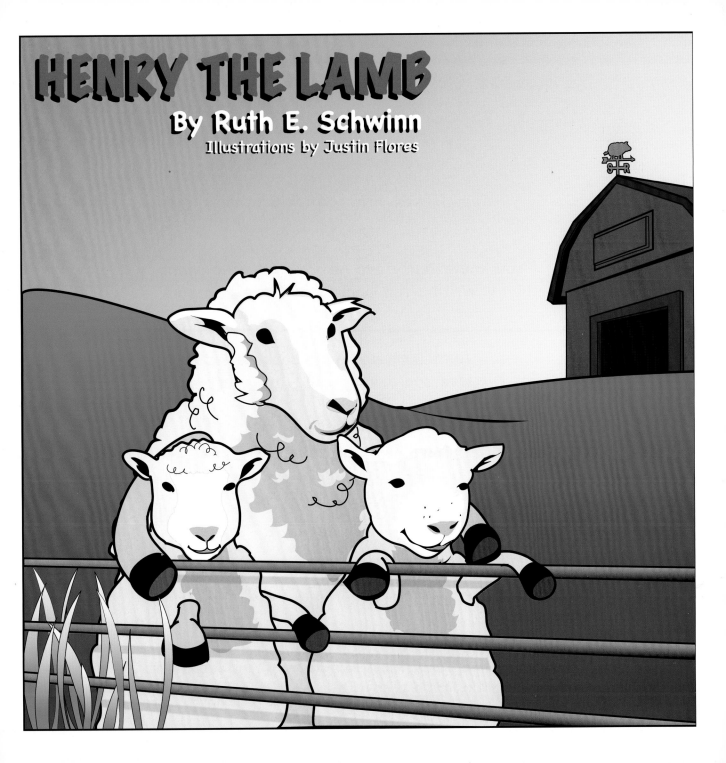

HENRY THE LAMB

By Ruth E. Schwinn

Illustrations by Justin Flores

If you knew Henry and he touched your heart,
then in writing this book you've played a part.

Lots of love to:
Aunt Terri and Aunt Barbara
for the love and devotion they gave to Henry

to Sandy and everyone else
who helps me follow my heart.

Henry was born at Pheasant Run Farm,

He was born in the cold. Just a few minutes old...
when his Mom had another! It was Burt, Henry's brother!

The Farmer came out at the end of the day. She was surprised to see Henry down there in the hay.

He had been flipped all around, all over the ground. He was dirty and wet and very upset!

So the farmer took Henry, took him out of the storm.
Took him into the house, where he would be nice and warm.

Henry shook and he shivered and finally warmed up.
He slept warm and cozy with Miss Patti pup.

He drank from a bottle with milk made for sheep.
But he wanted his Mom and he started to weep.

HENRY THE HOUSEPET

Happy Birthday!

..."Remember the day Burt showed off his short tail, then introduced Henry to Mimi and Dale?"...

Henry discovers life and adventures in the barnyard with all the other sheep.